The Mitten

Retold by Jim Aylesworth

Illustrated by Barbara McClintock

SCHOLASTIC INC.

New York Toronto London Auckland
Sydney Mexico City New Delhi Hong Kong

Once upon a time

there was a happy little boy who loved to play. Yes, he did.

In the spring, he loved to climb trees and peek in at baby birds.

In the summer, he loved to chase the golden butterflies.

In the autumn, he loved to play in piles of golden leaves.

And in the winter, he loved to play in the white, white snow.

And every winter, because she loved him, the little boy's grandmother would knit a great, warm woolen hat that he could pull down over his little ears,

a long, warm woolen scarf that he could wrap two times around his little neck,

and a pair of warm woolen mittens for his little hands. And on the cold, cold day of this story, the little boy dressed himself warmly in his hat and his scarf and his mittens, and he went outside to play.

He played,

and he played,

and he played.

But when at last he came inside, it was discovered that one of his mittens was lost.

"Oh, no!" said the little boy.

"Don't worry," said the grandmother. "We'll find it tomorrow. You've had enough of the cold for one day."

And because she loved him, she made him a mug of
steaming-hot chocolate.

In the meantime, just while the little boy was sipping his hot chocolate, a squirrel came along and saw the lost mitten lying on the snow.

"B-r-r-r-r-r-r-rrrrrrrrr!"
said the squirrel.
"My toes are cold as ice!
This mitten looks so cozy,
and warm toes would feel so nice!"

So the squirrel crawled into the little boy's mitten to warm his toes.

The squirrel found the mitten quite warm and very
comfortable, and soon he was so nice and toasty in there
that he fell sound asleep.

But just then, along came a rabbit.

"B-r-r-r-r-r-r-rrrrrrrr!"
said the rabbit.
"Let me come in."

"No room!" said the squirrel.
"Go away!"

"Please!" begged the rabbit.
"My toes are cold as ice!
Your mitten looks so cozy,
and warm toes would feel so nice!"

"Oh, okay!" said the squirrel.
"You can come in!"

And the rabbit crawled in.

It was a bit tight in there for two.

Nevertheless, with a little budging over, they were able to manage.

And very soon, they were nice and toasty warm, and they fell sound asleep.

But just then, along came a fox.

"B-r-r-r-r-r-r-rrrrrrrr!"
said the fox.
"Let me come in."

"No room!" said the rabbit.
"No room!" said the squirrel.
"GO AWAY!"

"Please!" begged the fox.
"My toes are cold as ice!
Your mitten looks so cozy,
and warm toes would feel so nice!"

"Oh, okay!" said the rabbit.
"Oh, okay!" said the squirrel.
"You can come in."

And the fox squeezed in.

It was really crowded in
there now with three.

Nevertheless, the mitten
stretched out enough . . .

and soon they were nice
and toasty warm.

But just when they had fallen sound
asleep, along came a bear.

"B-r-r-r-r-r-r-rrrrrrrrr!" said the bear.
"Let me come in."

"No room!" said the fox.
"No room!" said the rabbit.
"No room!" said the squirrel.
"GO AWAY!"

"Please!" begged the bear.
"My toes are cold as ice!
Your mitten looks so cozy,
and warm toes would feel *so* nice!"

"Oh, okay!" said the fox.
"Oh, okay!" said the rabbit.
"Oh, okay!" said the squirrel.
"You can come in."

The bear squeezed and pushed,

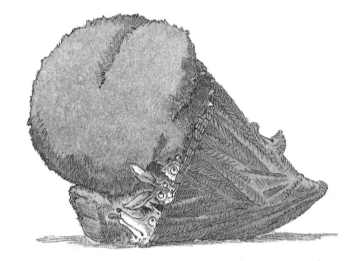

and squeezed and pushed,

and sque-e-e-ezed and pushed—
until at last . . .

. . . he got himself in.

It was very cramped in there with the four
of them all squished together like that.

Still, they were nice and toasty warm, and
soon they all fell sound asleep.

But just then, along came a little mouse.

"B-r-r-r-r-r-r-rrrrrrrrr!"
said the little mouse in a
teeny-tiny voice.

"Let me come in."

"No room!" said the bear.
"No room!" said the fox.
"No room!" said the rabbit.
"No room!" said the squirrel.
"GO AWAY!"

"Please!" begged the little mouse.
"My toes are cold as ice!
Your mitten looks so cozy,
and warm toes would feel so nice!"

"We can't!" said the bear.
"Too full!" said the fox.
"No way!" said the rabbit.
"Impossible!" said the squirrel.
"GO AWAY!"

"Ple-e-e-a-se!" said the little mouse.
"I'm just a little mouse."

"Oh, okay!" said the bear.
"Oh, okay!" said the fox.
"Oh, okay!" said the rabbit.
"Oh, okay!" said the squirrel.
"You can come in!"

And they all held their breath while the little mouse
carefully squeezed into a teeny-tiny spot.

And for a minute, all was well . . .

. . . until suddenly — the bear and the fox and the
rabbit and the squirrel all had to take a great big deep
breath of air. And as they did . . .

. . . the mitten BURST apart and spilled them
all out onto the snow!

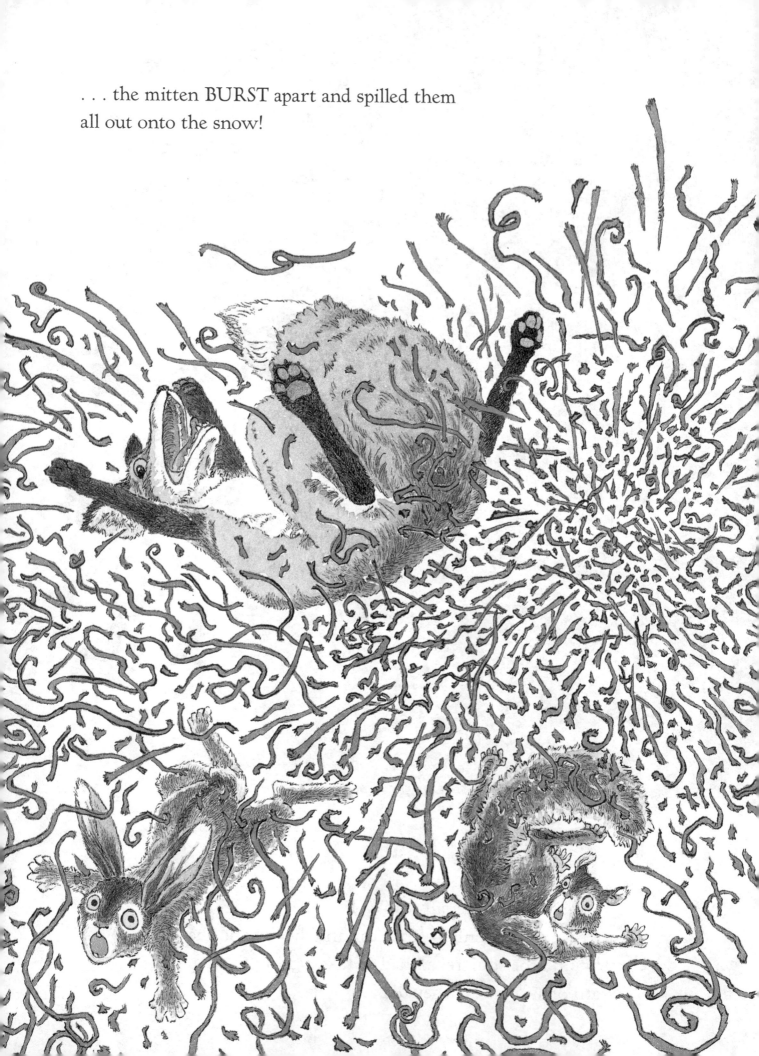

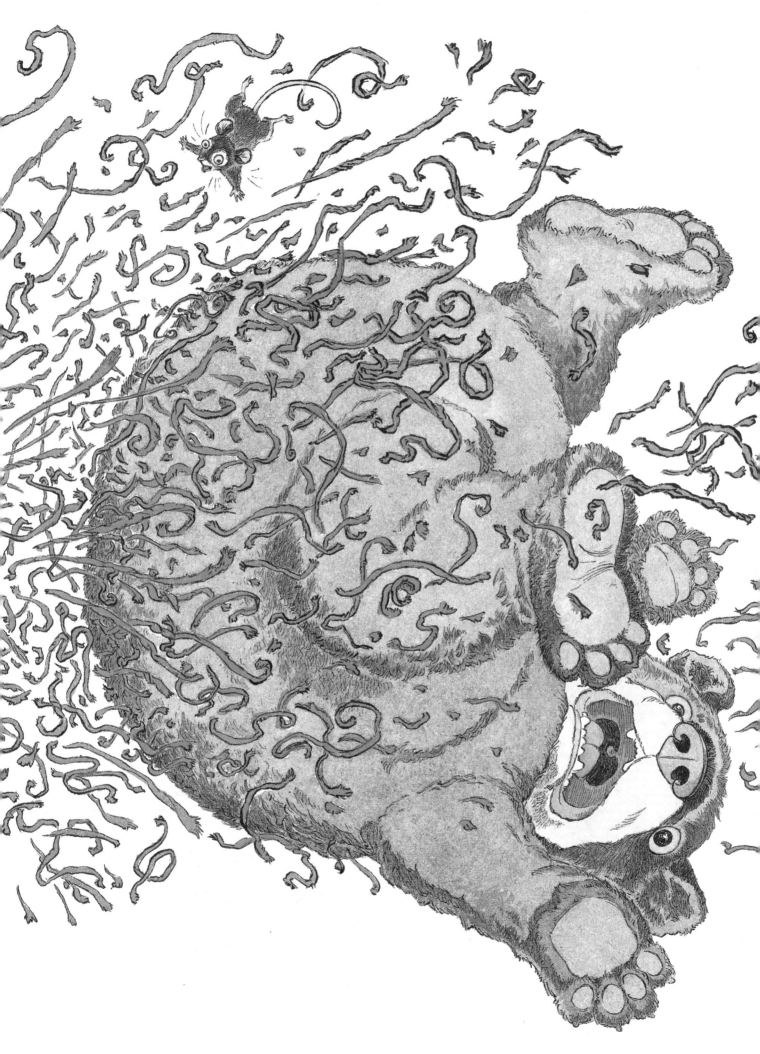

"What a shame!" said the bear.
"What a shame!" said the fox.
"What a shame!" said the rabbit.
"What a shame!" said the squirrel.
"Oh, it is!" said the little mouse.
"A terrible, terrible shame!"

Then one by one,

the mouse,

the bear,

the fox,

the rabbit,

and the squirrel

all went off to find another place to warm their toes.

In the morning, the little boy and his grandmother
went out looking for the lost mitten.

Soon, they came upon the bits and pieces of yarn
lying on the snow.

"What could have happened?"
asked the little boy.

"I have no idea!" said the
grandmother. "But don't worry,
I can knit another."

And because she loved him, that's *exactly* what she did.

To my dearest Sam, with love!—J.A.

For Tim—B.M.

This favorite old folk tale is believed to have originated in Ukraine. The motif is of too many characters crowding into a vessel until it bursts. There are many variants of this story, which have appeared in different countries. The vessels have included a hat, an earthenware jar, a house—and even the skull of a horse!

No part of this publication may be reproduced, stored in a retrieval system, or transmitted in any form or by any means, electronic, mechanical, photocopying, recording, or otherwise, without written permission of the publisher. For information regarding permission, write to Scholastic Inc., Attention: Permissions Department, 557 Broadway, New York, NY 10012.

ISBN: 978-0-545-22618-9

Text copyright © 2009 by Jim Aylesworth.
Illustrations copyright © 2009 by Barbara McClintock.
All rights reserved. Published by Scholastic Inc. SCHOLASTIC and associated logos are trademarks and/or registered trademarks of Scholastic Inc.

12 11 10 9 8 7 6 5 4 3 2 1   9 10 11 12 13 14/0

Printed in the U.S.A.   40

First Scholastic paperback printing, December 2009

Many thanks to Karen Van Rossem from the Scholastic library
for her help in locating earlier versions of the tale.

Handlettering by Kevin Pyle. The text was set in Hadriano Light.
The artwork was created with ink, gouache, and watercolor.

Book design by Lillie Mear and David Saylor